Lucy loved to tell stories.

She told deep-blue-sea stories to Mom,

flying-up-high-
in-the-sky
stories to Dad,

and magic stories to her
little brother, Jamie.

But best of all were the bedtime stories she told to Bear.
Lucy loved bedtime. She'd hug Bear and whisper stories until
they fell asleep.

But poor Jamie hated bedtime. He'd toss and turn
with Floppy Rabbit and see things in the shadows on the
ceiling.

One night when Jamie was wide awake again, Lucy told him, "Bear can't sleep either. We need to find the Dreamtime Fairies. They'll help us."

So Lucy, Bear, Jamie, and Floppy Rabbit
flew far away across the ocean to
the land where the fairies live.

They landed on a rock.
"Turtle!" said Jamie.

"We can't sleep," said Lucy, "so we're looking for the fairies."
"The Dreamtime Fairies?" said Turtle. "They're very shy.
You'll have to look very hard to find them.
Turtles sleep in the sun — why don't you?"
"We could try," Lucy said,
and they all lay
in the sun.

Turtle fell asleep, and Bear and
Floppy Rabbit fell asleep, but …
"Too hot!" said Jamie.

"Come on," said Lucy, "let's find the fairies."

Jamie heard something moving
high up in the trees.
"Tiger!" he said.
"We can't sleep," said Lucy, "so
we're looking for the fairies."

"The Dreamtime Fairies?" said Tiger. "They live far away in the forest. Tigers sleep in trees — why don't you?"
"We could try," said Lucy, and they climbed up, shut their eyes, and rocked in the branches.

Tiger fell asleep, Bear and Floppy Rabbit fell asleep, and even Turtle fell asleep, but … "Too high!" said Jamie.

"Come on," said Lucy, "let's find the fairies."

They saw two eyes shining in a deep, dark cave.

"Foxy!" shouted Jamie. "We can't sleep," said Lucy, "so we're looking for the fairies."

"The Dreamtime Fairies?" said Foxy. "They live in the shadows, down in the darkness. Foxes sleep in cozy, dark holes—why don't you?"

"Too dark!" said Jamie.

"But we'll have to go into the shadows to find the fairies," said Lucy. "Come on, we'll hold hands!"

So Lucy, Jamie, Bear, Floppy Rabbit, Turtle, Tiger, and Foxy followed the path as it twisted and turned. Down into the forest, down into the darkness, deep down to where the shadows grow.

Jamie thought he heard something in the shadows. . . .
"Shh!" whispered Lucy.
They all stood absolutely still,
hardly daring to breathe.

Jamie thought he saw
something in the shadows. . . .

"Fairies," whispered Jamie.
First there was one shimmer,
then another, and another. . . .

until soon the fairies were all around, swooping and dancing and laughing.

Everyone danced and played as the fairies fluttered and twinkled.

"There's no need to be afraid of the shadows, Jamie," said Lucy, "because that's where the Dreamtime Fairies fly."

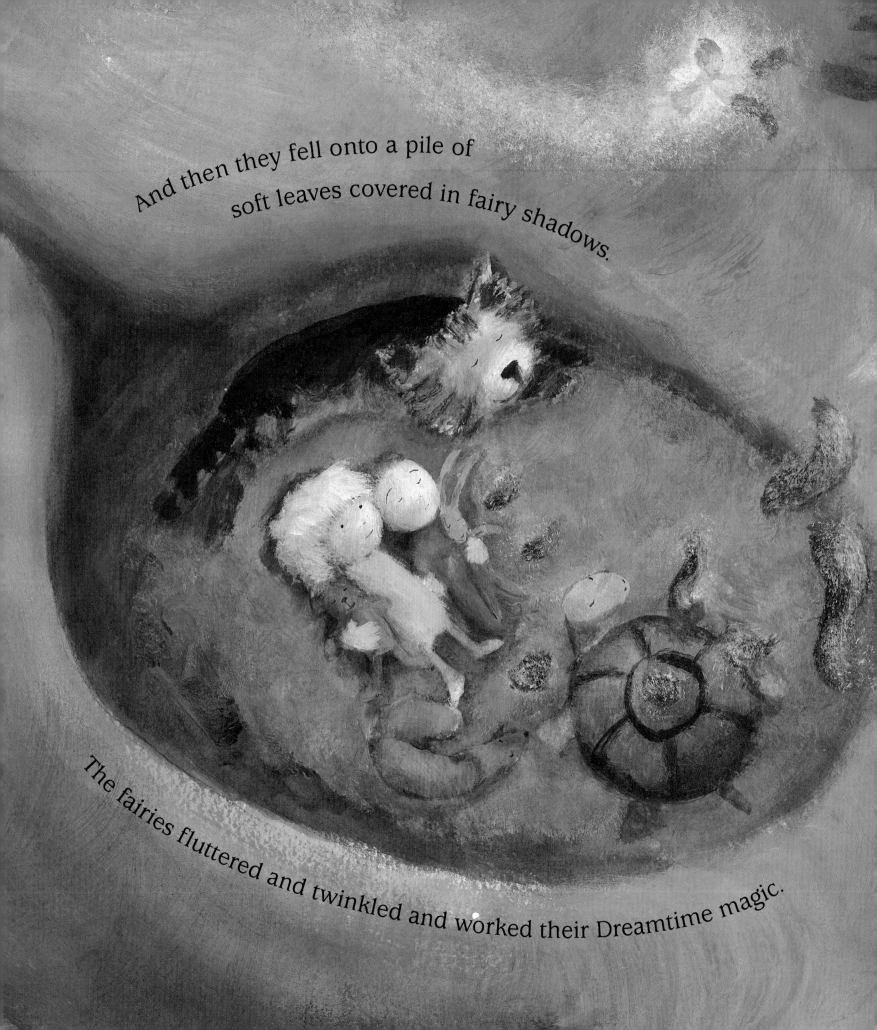

And then they fell onto a pile of
soft leaves covered in fairy shadows.

The fairies fluttered and twinkled and worked their Dreamtime magic.

And one by one, first Jamie, then
Floppy Rabbit, then Turtle, Tiger, and Foxy,
then Bear, and then finally Lucy...

gently drifted into the magic
of sweet dreams.

Zzzzzzzz